Underground Town

Story by Melaina Faranda

Illustrations by Lukas Thelin

Underground Town

Text: Melaina Faranda
Publishers: Tania Mazzeo and Eliza Webb
Series consultant: Amanda Sutera
Hands on Heads Consulting
Editor: Jess Mackay
Project editor: Annabel Smith
Designer: Jess Kelly
Project designer: Danielle Maccarone
Illustrations: Lukas Thelin
Production controller: Renee Tome

NovaStar

ISBN 978 0 17 033514 0

Cengage Learning Australia
Level 5, 80 Dorcas Street
Southbank VIC 3006 Australia
Phone: 1300 790 853
Email: aust.nelsonprimary@cengage.com

For learning solutions, visit **cengage.com.au**

Printed in China by 1010 Printing International Ltd
1 2 3 4 5 6 7 29 28 27 26 25

Nelson acknowledges the Traditional Owners and Custodians of the lands of all First Nations Peoples. We pay respect to Elders past and present, and extend that respect to all First Nations Peoples today.

Contents

Chapter 1

Camel Spit

The cameleer called over to where Dad was sorting their luggage. "You might want to tell your son to be careful–"

The warning came too late. A camel drew back its soft, rubbery lips to reveal long, yellow teeth that yawned open before it projected steaming brownish spit straight at Dimi's face.

Dimi gagged at the disgusting stench of camel cud. He swiped frantically at the sticky strands of spit. It was everywhere: on his cheeks and in his hair. A swarm of flies, already intolerable, crowded all over the smelly slime.

Satisfied, the camel lowered its long neck to the ground, where it knelt, knees hobbled, in a clump of seven other camels.

All Dimi had wanted to do was touch the hump, because the cameleer had said there were no bones in it – it was just a giant lump of fat that could be used as energy for the camel to walk for days or weeks without eating. As for drinking, Dimi had already seen how each beast was able to drain bucket after bucket of water in one sitting.

Mama rushed over with a handkerchief, lifting from her hat the net veil that protected against the swarming flies. Her large, dark eyes showed sympathy as she helped wipe Dimi clean. "Oh, Dimitrios! *Kardia mou*. My heart. My miracle."

Dad chuckled, along with the rest of the men, from where he was keeping an eye on the cameleers loading the family's precious supplies, including picks, shovels, buckets, ropes and chains. "No need to fuss over the boy, Daphne."

Dimi stomped off, his cheeks burning, not only from the glaring sunlight. He didn't want his father to see how upset he was.

Bill was a hero from World War II, with a box full of medals awarded to him for daring and bravery. Less than thirteen years before, Dad had lived in the trenches, surviving bombs and being shot at. He'd finally escaped from the brutal prisoner-of-war camp where he'd been held captive by the Italians.

Dimi's parents both believed Bill had been protected by the evil-eye charm Daphne had given him when they first met in a military hospital on the Greek island of Crete. He was a foreign soldier, she a girl from a local village. It was a smooth, blue-and-white pendant in the shape of a round eye with a glossy black pupil at the centre, intended to keep harm away, including other people's nasty intentions or "evil eyes". Whether that was true or not, Dad had survived and still wore the charm around his neck. Next to that, a bit of camel spit was nothing.

If they were still in the city, Dimi would have fled to the grey, rubbish-strewn beach nearby, where gulls shrieked above the freezing sea. But here, there wasn't anywhere for him to go aside from the shanty railway siding with its splintered silver weatherboards and rusting iron roof. The same flat desert, with scatterings of reddish gravel the size of coins to cricket balls, stretched as far as he could see in every direction.

A week ago, they had still been living in a place where the grass grew so quickly Dimi had to borrow the neighbour's push mower once a week. In the backyard, Mama's vegetable gardens flourished with tomatoes, eggplants, okra and green beans.

One week ago, seemingly endless rain had fallen from a cloudy sky, only breaking long enough for Dimi to play a final game of cricket with the other kids in the street.

And one week ago, Dad worked his final day down at the docks. He had grown tired of being treated badly by his bosses, the poor conditions, and being expected to drop everything and work overtime for no extra pay.

Only two months before that, Mama had laid the embroidered cream tablecloth they had brought with them to the new country when they had sailed there from Crete six years ago. She had set the table for dinner, Dad and Dimi's favourite – moussaka: a delicious cheese-covered dish of tomato, eggplant and lamb mince. Dad had been quiet, until suddenly his knife and fork clattered to his untouched plate.

"I just don't know how much longer I can keep working on the waterfront," Dad announced.

"It was bad enough in the war, being in the trenches and taking orders from those so-and-sos, but the bosses down at the docks are worse.

They are bullies who are all about the dollar, and no matter how hard you and I work, Daphne, we never seem to get ahead."

Mama glanced at the uneaten moussaka.

"But what will you do instead?" she asked carefully. "We need money to pay the rent and to save for a house of our own."

Dimi knew that Mama dreamed most about having a place where she could grow not only vegetables but a lemon tree. Somewhere they could never be moved on from. His parents rarely spoke about the war, but Dimi recalled enough gossip amongst the older people from when he had been a small boy to know that Mama had nearly starved as a teenager during the war. She had stolen eggs straight from beneath a neighbour's hen and grazed on wild grasses like an animal. Her body had become so wasted she believed she might never be able to have children, and her family home had been destroyed in the fighting. All that was left of a household once filled with laughter and the aromas of good cooking was a pile of rubble and a lemon tree.

Dad had also been what he called "a walking skeleton" in a prisoner-of-war camp. What they both wanted more than anything was a quiet life of peace; a place with no landlord threatening a rent rise; and for Dimi, their miracle child, to have better opportunities than they had.

"At the rate we're going, there won't ever be enough money to do that," Dad said quietly.

For all Mama scrimped, something always seemed to come along that ate into those precious savings. Dad's truck broke down. It was fixed at great expense and then promptly broke down again. A mysterious winter illness struck Dimi, which meant that Mama had to stop working at the milk bar while still paying for Dr Hall's many house calls.

Mama's shoulders slumped at this reminder, and Dad reached into his pocket and unfolded a newspaper article. As Dad laid it on the tablecloth, his blue eyes were bright with excitement.

"It'll take us years to get ahead. But there's been a big opal find in the desert out back. Worth millions. Someone struck it lucky. Reckon if we get out there early enough, we could too."

Chapter 2

Stars and Stories

Riding camels across the desert to an opal-mining town was very different from riding donkeys along the craggy coastlines Dimi only had faint memories of from living in Crete. One of the cameleers had told him that camels were also known as ships of the desert. It made sense, not only because of all the goods they transported, but also because their swaying walk from side to side felt like being at sea.

The camels plodded under their loads across the sun-baked desert, and the rhythmic rocking caused Dimi to give up batting away the flies and nearly fall asleep in his saddle.

By the time the sun sank behind the horizon, casting a soft, pink light over the endless stony plains, he was almost too tired to eat.

Dinner was corned beef from tins opened with a key, and a bland mix of flour and water one of the men shaped into balls around sticks to toast over a fire.

Dimi wrinkled his nose and forced himself to chew the tinned meat and charred dough. He was used to Mama's cooking in which the meat – usually lamb – was slow cooked, tender and flavoured with garlic and oregano.

Later, wrapped in a cocoon of rough woollen blankets, Dimi curled close to Mama. Her soft arm circled him as she whispered in Greek one of her many stories of the gods and goddesses, before falling asleep mid-sentence. The sweltering heat of the day rapidly cooled into an icy desert night. Snores punctuated the silence, accompanied by occasional grunts and sighs from the camels.

Overhead, stars sparkled like a river of gemstones in the velvety darkness.

Dimi scanned for the constellations Mama had showed him, especially Taurus. The Taurus constellation was named after the Minotaur – the hideous man-eating beast. Half-human and half-bull, it was kept hidden in an underground labyrinth, deep beneath the palace of Knossos in Crete. Mama had told him that whenever he spotted Taurus in the night sky, he should remember her homeland and the place where he too had been born.

They would have stayed in Crete, except that the Greek civil war had only continued to intensify the devastation of World War II. Despite leaving behind her own mother and everyone and everything she had ever known, it had been Mama who had insisted they move to Dad's country. There would be more opportunities there and she wanted Dimi to have a better life.

In the six years they had lived in the city close to the docks, Mama had made the best of it.

She grew their vegetables, brought home leftovers from the milk bar where she worked, sewed and patched their clothes, and denied herself anything new, even when Dad insisted. But somehow, they could still never seem to get ahead.

After Dad made his announcement that they would be moving out west to the desert to stake an opal-mining claim and make their fortune, Dimi had eavesdropped on the fiercely whispered argument behind their bedroom door.

“What kind of life will we be giving our son?” Mama demanded. “There will be no school there for a twelve-year-old boy!”

No school? Dimi felt a rush of excitement. School was a place with hard wooden benches and stern teachers who rarely smiled and made everyone repeat the times tables. They never told the types of wonderful stories Mama did about gods and goddesses and heroes and monsters.

“He can do school by correspondence,” Dad replied.

Dimi’s heart sank again.

He could imagine Dad’s blue eyes shining as he said, “C’mon, Daphne, since when have you or I ever been afraid to take a risk? It’s a gamble, but we both know we can’t take anything for granted. One moment it’s here. The next, someone’s bombed it to bits. We’ll try to strike it lucky with opal and then we’ll be out of there in no time and set for life.”

But when the camel team finally pulled into the makeshift mining town, Dimi grimly took in the place they would be calling their new home. Strike it lucky? It seemed unlikely.

Chapter 3

Underground Town

The place was a barren moonscape of stony ground and pink-orange rock littered with rusting heaps of abandoned and broken machinery. Deep holes surrounded by heaped pyramids of dirt pocked the earth. Entrances had been carved into the sides of small mounds, with doors set into them. Some had brush shelters for shade. Above them, dotting the otherwise bare stone hillocks, were pipes and tin drums with metal caps poking up like bizarre metallic mushrooms. Dad explained they were air vents.

Dad scowled at the dogs, with their ribs poking through mangy coats, randomly wandering about. For as long as Dimi could recall, his father had hated dogs.

Apart from the dogs and Reg, the man in

charge of allocating and administering mining claims and the town's "unofficial mayor", there was not a soul to be seen.

"All sorts live out here," Reg said. "People from across the world hoping to get rich. One thing they've got in common is being struck by opal fever."

"But where is everyone?" Dimi asked, swiping at the flies that swarmed around his face and crawled into the corners of his mouth and eyes.

Reg pointed directly beneath their feet. "Under the ground."

Dimi shuddered. "Like the Minotaur's labyrinth or Hades?"

"Don't know wotcha talking about, kid."

"The underworld!" Dimi insisted.

Dad squeezed his shoulder and whispered, "Don't think this fella is so up on his Greek mythology, son." He winked at Mama, but she didn't seem to notice.

A deep line scored itself across the bridge of Mama's nose and dismay showed in her large, dark eyes. She wiped the sweat from her forehead and gestured into the stony wasteland. "Where are we going to live?"

Reg beamed. "As it happens, you're in luck. Tito, one of the older miners, fell down a shaft and banged himself up bad. The flying doctor took him to a hospital in the city and his daughter won't let him come back out here. His dugout's been empty ever since. It's a good, solid one, no need to worry about the roof collapsing in on you overnight."

He added, "It's no good just having single blokes out here. What we need is more families – women and kids to make it a real community. We've got some other Italians here, too."

Dad frowned. "My wife is from Greece."

Reg shrugged. "Same part of the world."

But even Dimi knew that there was no love lost between Dad and Italians. During the war, the Italians, together with the German Nazis, had invaded Greece. They had imprisoned Dad in the war camp.

"You'll want to get friendly with Mrs Stein," Reg said to Mama. "She'll know anything worth knowing in this town. She runs the post office and operates the radio."

"There's a post office here?" Dimi couldn't hide his astonishment.

"Highlight of the week when the mail comes in." Reg regarded Dimi for a moment before adding, "That's when school correspondence will arrive."

Dimi pointed to the heaped pyramids of dirt.

It wasn't like back in the city, with its rows of houses and numbered mailboxes. "How do they know where to deliver?"

Reg gave a bark of laughter. "They don't! That's why everyone gathers at the post office once a week to collect letters and goods. This is an underground town." He stamped his foot to draw their attention to the ground. "You'd be surprised what's sitting under here. Not just opals. There are churches, a general store – everything you could want.

"But, as I was saying, Tito's place is empty. And you can have it for as long as his daughter can keep him from coming back here. If she's half as stubborn as the old man, it'll be some while before he gets back to gouge. That's what we call digging for opal around here – gouging."

Reg's expression became dreamy. "Thing about gouging for opal is that it gets under your skin. Days and weeks of slogging and hauling buckets of mullock – that's the broken-down rocks you'll be hauling to the surface – for that one precious glint to make it all worthwhile." He gestured across the rocky nothingness. "See that door over there? The one with the brushwood screen for shade? That one's yours."

Chapter 4

Troglodytes

Inside the dugout, sheltered from incessant flies and warm gusting air, it was quiet and still. There were no windows, and apart from daylight spilling through the open door there was only a tiny ring of white light visible through the vent above.

"Keeps the fresh air circulating," Reg said.

"It's so much cooler in here!" Dimi's eyes gradually adjusted to the irregularly shaped space while Reg told them how the shadowy dugout had been hacked into the hill with the use of explosives and a pick and shovel. Ledges and alcoves had been carved into the bare rock walls.

"Same temperature in here year-round," Reg said proudly. "Let me tell you, it makes a big difference from the bad old days of camping under canvas. Gets so hot out here in the summer a gouger can easily go mad and die."

Dad surveyed the rounded ceiling of pocked rock above. "Why are there no braces or props to hold all this up?"

"Rare kind of rock out here," Reg answered proudly. "Means there's no need for support or surrounds."

"This is just like the troglodytes," Dimi said.

Reg raised his eyebrows questioningly.

"They were the people from ancient times who lived in caves and ate lizards and things," Dimi explained. "Mama told me about them."

Mama didn't respond. She stood with hands on hips, peering through the gloom at the thick layer of dust coating the rickety kitchen table and bits of furniture cobbled from old wooden crates. Scattered throughout the dugout were randomly tossed piles of what looked – judging by a hideous crusting – to be unrinsed tin cans. It seemed hazardous for Dimi to move, as if the stacks of rubbish might suddenly come toppling down.

Reg didn't seem to notice Mama's despair as he replied to Dimi, "Well, I guess there are plenty of lizards and snakes around here. But no need to be eating them. There's the general store.

And once a week the men from the cattle station will cart in butchered steers for you to buy your meat."

He gestured around the room. "Tito wasn't exactly houseproud, but there are a couple of shafts we use for disposing of our garbage.
Reg avoided Mama's eyes. "I'll point them out so you can give the place a tidy up and get properly settled. You'll want to see the bedrooms."

Two smaller, craggy stone rooms were annexed to the large one through crudely cut rock hallways. One of the rooms contained a sagging double bed. Horsehair and straw stuck out from the mattress in prickly clumps. Everything was covered with the same thick film of dust.

"What about water?" Mama suddenly piped up, her voice bordering on shrill. "How do I keep things clean?"

Reg pointed to a barrel in the corner by the entrance.

"There's a water truck that comes once a week from out of town. That's an improvement. It used to be brought in by camels and carts. Just a warning – until you get used to it – water is what you're going to miss most out here, and it's not cheap. And here's some more free advice: people can be funny about money here. They're the best of friends when no one's got any but when the colour shows in the rock, some people will go crazy and do anything to get their hands on it."

"What colour *is* opal?" Dimi asked.

"It depends," Reg said. "If you're talking about fire opal, there's a lot of oranges and reds. Black opals can show every colour of the rainbow. Crystal opal, especially the greens and blues, can be like little planets. Then there's sifting through all the worthless grey and white potch."

He looked dreamy before adding, "Greed for opal can be like a fever. If you strike it lucky, you might want to keep that to yourself for a bit. It's not unknown for some to do a sneaky night shift to raid another man's claim. We call them ratters."

Reg fixed Dimi with a serious stare. "Another thing, and for the young man especially – you'll all want to be careful where you walk. This whole area is covered in shafts. Easy place to fall into a hole and vanish. Don't walk around at night without a lamp. And whatever you do, *never* walk backwards."

Reg grinned and nodded to Dad. "With all this talk, guess you'll want to see your claim."

Dimi wanted desperately to follow the men to further inspect their claim. Maybe they would find opals on the first day! Then they could get out of here sooner.

Instead, he was drafted into tidying up. Mama tore an old frock into rag strips and, using these and a small brush-broom she had thought to add to their supplies, they dusted and swept and wiped. Mama barely eked out a spoonful of water each time to wet the cloth. They shook out the blankets and beat the solitary threadbare rug that covered a small patch of the rock floor.

Mama scoured tin plates and mugs before unpacking their own, while Dimi fetched each disgusting, unrinsed tin can and put them outside the sun-bleached timber of the front door.

By the time Dad returned, the dugout was, if still not entirely clean, clear enough to walk into and through without stumbling over scattered furniture and tin cans.

Dimi had discovered a dusty tin of kerosene in what was to be his bedroom. The two kerosene lamps had been wiped clean and now cast a warm, golden glow over their new home.

Mama covered the old table with their thickly embroidered tablecloth. Its creamy colour was unlikely to remain so here. They were also eating sardines from cans, but Mama insisted on putting them on a plate. She sniffed. "Just because we now live in a cave like troglodytes doesn't mean that we have to act like them too. Tomorrow, we will get you started on your correspondence school, Dimi. You have already missed a week."

Dimi sighed, spearing a sardine with his fork.

Dad laughed. "Give the kid a break. We've just arrived, Daphne. Besides, I'm going to need a bit of help getting the mine set up."

Chapter 5

Dogs

It was strange how the more Dimi observed the barren desert with its rusty gravel surface, the more he noticed that it wasn't really empty. As he followed Dad to their claim, small flocks of brightly coloured birds rose from silvery grey bushes that clung to clefts in the sandstone. Stray dogs lay panting beneath a solitary gnarled tree in what appeared to be a dried-up creek.

The occasional flatbed truck, loaded with mining equipment, inched along rutted tracks, kicking up white clouds of dust in its wake. In the distance, men looked like ants, hauling up buckets of rocks from mine shafts and sifting and noodling through the mullock heaps.

Their mining claim was an allotted plot of bare earth, smaller than the backyard Mama had grown vegetables in.

As Dimi watched Dad pace the pegged perimeter, a man from the neighbouring claim only 50 or so metres away winched himself up from one of the many shafts that pocked the plains. His dark eyes shone beneath eyebrows white with dust. He called out with a voice that was musical and heavily accented. “I had wondered who would be coming!”

Picking his way through the mullock heaps, the man smiled and stuck out his hand to Dad. “I’m Francesco. People call me Frank. If you need any help –”

To Dimi’s astonishment, Dad gave a curt nod beneath the broad brim of his hat and, ignoring the outstretched hand, marched past.

Frank stood, his smile tightening, before shrugging and returning to sift through a heap of broken rock.

Dad paced in the centre of their claim and gestured to Dimi to hand him one of the picks he had sharpened only that morning. “We’ll dig the shaft here.”

“How do you know where to dig?” Dimi asked in a low voice, still embarrassed by Dad’s response to Frank.

Dad grinned. "We've got to start somewhere."

The day was exhausting, with Dad swinging the pick to break up the rock and Dimi responsible for shovelling dirt far away from what would be the entrance to their mine. As the hole grew deeper, Dad lowered himself inside and Dimi reached to lift the buckets and dump the mullock, all the while looking for a telltale gleam of colour.

"Won't be long before we can drill and use some explosives to speed up the process," Dad said.

Dimi nodded, excited. Mama had said the name for those explosives – dynamite – had come from *dynamis*, the Greek word for "power".

At sunset, mindful of the dangers of the encroaching dark, they staggered home across a moonscape bathed in rosy, golden light. Blisters stung the soft pads between Dimi's thumbs and fingers. Covered in dust and stumbling with exhaustion, he waited until they were far enough away from their claim to ask something that had bothered him all day. "Why didn't you shake Frank's hand, Dad?"

Dad shook his head. "Moved back home from halfway across the world to get further away from them," he muttered.

"Get away from who?"

"Italians. Almost as bad as the Germans. They were the reason I ended up in the prison camp. Mark my words, Dimi – Frank, Francesco, whatever his name is, can't be trusted."

Dimi gingerly touched one of the swelling blisters on his palm. "But Dad, the war was before I was even born!"

Dad said nothing.

Dimi repeated, "Dad, it's not the war now."

Dad stared into the distance, as if he was looking back in time. He stopped and slowly lifted his shirt to reveal strange, silvery marks on his stomach and ribs.

Dimi froze. He had never seen Dad without a shirt on before. And the marks looked like scars from ... bites.

"When I tried to escape the prison camp, they set the dogs on me."

"Who set the dogs on you?"

Dad shook his head and spat. "Who do you think? The guards."

They fell silent again. Just before they arrived at the dugout, their boots crunching over the gravel, Dad said quietly, "You're not to tell your mother I showed you."

Mama flung open the door. A warm glow spilled from the entrance as she rushed to take their hats and line the picks and shovels up against the wall, then usher them inside. When she asked Dimi how his day had been he didn't tell her about Frank, or the blisters.

Chapter 6

Lucky

It was difficult to know who made up the town's population with everyone largely living and working underground. Although it was autumn, and far from the peak of the summer heat Reg had warned them about, few people were visible. If not for the mullock pyramids increasing in size around the mine shafts, it sometimes seemed to Dimi as if there was hardly anyone in town at all.

This changed on the day when the mail was delivered. People came out in force. It felt like a celebration. Trucks driven by miners working in surrounding opal fields thundered into town. As Mama shyly introduced herself to other women, Dimi saw a few other children running around kicking a football. They all looked younger than him.

Reg took Mama and Dad to meet the postmistress overseeing the occasion. “It’s good to make a friend of Mrs Stein. She’s the one with the medical box and radio. If anything out here goes wrong, we’re miles from help. Someone gets bit by a snake, busts an appendix or falls down a shaft – it’s Mrs Stein who radioes the flying doctor service. She’s the heart of this place.”

Mrs Stein waved her hand dismissively at Reg. “Bah. He makes me sound more important than I am.” She spoke with a thick German accent.

Immediately, Dimi sensed his parents stiffening. Dad grasped Mama’s hand and pulled her close. He grabbed Dimi with his spare hand and tugged them both out into the surrounding scrum.

Later, in the dugout, with thick rock separating their rooms, Dimi could only hear muffled sounds of his parents’ discussion. But the next week, on mail day, Dad decided to continue working on the mine, while Mama remained, sewing, in the dugout. Dimi was sent alone, to check if he had received any schoolwork from the correspondence school.

To his relief, nothing had arrived. It meant he could spend more time with Dad working on the claim.

On his way back to the dugout, swiping irritably at the swarming flies, Dimi heard a whimper. It came from beneath the rusted hulk of a decaying car. As he approached, the whimpering turned into a whine that tugged at his heart.

Two round, dark eyes gleamed from a dirt hollow beneath the bonnet. Dimi gently reached his hand in to where a tan-coloured puppy's stumpy little tail thudded in the dust. He scooped it out from beneath the car. As he held the quivering creature against his chest, Dimi felt the puppy's rapid heartbeat.

Where was its mother? Was she skulking about, scavenging amongst rubbish scraps, looking for food? He scanned the area. There was nothing but rock and the closed doors of dugouts keeping the flies and dust out. Dimi knew he should leave the puppy where he found it. Dad loathed dogs and had finally told Dimi why, but it was impossible to ignore the shining brown eyes and grateful licks.

"Dimi!" Mama called, from where she sat darning socks that were constantly worn through by his and Dad's boots. "Did any of the schoolwork arrive?"

"No, Mama, but something else did." Dimi emerged from the shadows into the light of the kerosene lamp and held up the squirming puppy.

Mama's eyes momentarily lit up. Then she shook her head. "Oh Dimi, my heart, we cannot keep it. Your father ..."

"Please, Mama! Maybe we could feed him before Dad gets back from the mine. He's hungry."

Mama shook her head even while she rose to fetch a knife to carve off slivers from a joint of meat they had bought from the butcher's cart.

The puppy devoured it, then promptly fell into a deep slumber in a nest of Mama's mending.

When Dad returned at sunset and the door opened, the puppy uttered high little yips of warning. Then, tumbling over its own paws, it scrabbled over Dad's boots to lunge at him with ecstatic licks. Dad stared. "What on–"

Mama quickly crossed the floor to kiss him on his dusty cheek. "Dimi found it under some rubbish. The dog will die out there by itself." Before he could say anything, she added quietly, "Our boy will get lonely out here. He needs a friend."

Dad was no match for Mama, and seeing that she had succeeded, Dimi announced, "I think we should call him Lucky."

Chapter 7

The Colour

In seven months, they had still not made a "lucky strike". They had come across the potch that Reg had spoken about – worthless white opal, and some common rough opal that could be sold to the dealers for small sums – but were yet to discover anything precious.

The shaft was now deep, with the cavern below bellying out and leading into different tunnels. Dad didn't mind the work. He said he was used to being in trenches and when all was said and done, he preferred to be his own boss. Mama kept the dugout as neat and clean as she could and had started a business mending miners' clothes.

In the evenings, occasionally caught by the mining bug that had bitten Dad and Dimi, she laid down her sewing to help sift through buckets of mullock that Dimi carted home.

There were times, too, when Mama joined Dimi up on the surface above their mine, to noodle through the rubble of the mullock heaps for something of value. While they noodled, Lucky, who was already growing from a little round ball of cuteness into a longer, rangier young dog, wandered and wagged his way across the claims, without any respect for ownership.

This included their neighbour, Frank, who always greeted Lucky with friendly pats. It only highlighted to Dimi how Frank and his father never greeted each other. At first, Dimi had found it embarrassing and odd. They could each hear the muffled booming whenever either man detonated explosives and the creaking of each other's windlasses as they hauled mullock from the shafts.

Dad didn't trust either him or Dimi being lowered from the tripod windlass and had decided upon rope ladders, which they clambered up and down.

There had been times when they really could have benefited from another man's help. Frank had even tried to offer it once or twice, but Dad had declined, tight-lipped and determined to keep a wary distance.

His parents were the same with Mrs Stein in the post office when they were forced to go there to collect larger objects and parcels. Even though she always had a smile for Dimi when he posted and collected his correspondence school packages, Mama and Dad kept their transactions, and any chat surrounding them, to a barely polite minimum.

During the winter, it was possible to rug up and sort through the mullock heaps. Spring had brought more warmth and it was also bearable. But as the summer months crept closer, the heat intensified until it was too dangerous to be outside for too long. Mama retreated to the dugout to sew. Their savings had dwindled to the extent that it was Mama's mending that enabled them to pay for food.

Dimi wished he could help, too, but he was only allowed to join Dad down in the mine when he had completed his schoolwork. He had grown used to the work. His arms were strong and the thick pads of callus that had formed on his palms and fingers meant he rarely suffered from blisters.

The walk back and forth to the mine beneath the hot, cloudless sky was punishing. Descending the rope ladders was a reward, even if it meant the constant back-breaking labour of swinging a pick and shovelling shale into a bucket.

Sometimes, excited by a possible glimmer in the rock, Dad and Dimi worked through the night to follow it. In the tunnels that led from the main shaft, night or day made no difference; they always needed kerosene lamps or candles for light. Candles were also useful for showing where there was bad air: if there wasn't enough oxygen, the flames would dwindle and be snuffed out. Periodically, they would hold the candles closer to the rock to scan for any faint gleam.

Sometimes veins would simply vanish, but the colour could also be hidden in pipes or kernels of rock.

It was on one of those nights, when Dad swung the pick and a shower of rocks tumbled to the cave floor, that Dimi spotted a tell-tale glint.

Trembling, he picked up one of the stones and held it out to Dad. The two of them stared.

There were colours – a brilliant shimmer in the flicker of candlelight. The two of them scrabbled to gather the rest of the fallen rock from Dad's strike into the bucket, and then they hauled it home under the cover of darkness.

Chapter 8

Safe

Inside the dugout, Mama was still sewing the heap of mending work that had rapidly built up around her. Lucky lay curled at her feet.

"Daphne, bring the lamp!" Dad called.

Mama frowned as he tipped the bucket straight onto her embroidered tablecloth, but Dimi grinned at the barely suppressed glee in his father's voice. "You're going to want to see this."

The three of them huddled over the spread of rocks. Threaded through them was a wonderland of colour.

Dad breathed out slowly. "We made a lucky strike." The excitement was so immense that they barely slept that night.

With Mama and Lucky keeping guard over their haul at home, Dad and Dimi returned to the mine in the morning to explore the seam in different directions, but they found no more obvious veins of colour.

To avoid word getting out, it was decided Dad should travel to the city, a journey that would take a week or two, and try to sell their opal directly to jewellers. They couldn't risk asking for anyone else's advice and, as far as Dad and Mama were concerned, the radio was off limits for making enquiries – especially with it being operated by a German.

It was best if Dad sold their find soon rather than risk having it stolen. They agreed that if anyone asked, the story Mama and Dimi would tell was that he needed to go to the city for an operation.

The weather was too hot even for camels, and Dad arranged to pay for a lift out with the supply truck.

"Can I keep mining while you're gone?" Dimi asked.

For a moment, it seemed as if Dad might agree. There was a light in his blue eyes that shone brighter than the evil-eye charm around his neck. Opal fever.

Mama frowned and sternly shook her head. “No, Dimi. You’ll need to do your schoolwork. The mine can wait until your father returns.”

“But what about the ratters?”

Dad had worried aloud about the possibility that someone would raid their mine while he was gone. He never said who that ratter might be, but it was obvious to Dimi who he meant.

Dad looked torn. “We’ve kept our find to ourselves the best we could. We’ll just have to take our chances until I’m back. You can go to the claim to keep an eye out, and check that everything’s the same.”

Dimi nodded, knowing Dad meant keeping an eye on their neighbour, Frank.

“But son, you’re *not* to go down the mine. It’s too dangerous to be in there by yourself.”

Regarding Dimi for a long moment, Dad did something he had never done before. He tugged the cord knotted around the glass evil-eye charm, then slipped it over his head and put it around Dimi’s neck. Dimi savoured the warmth of where it had lain against Dad’s own chest.

“To keep you safe,” Dad murmured.

Chapter 9

The Dark

At first, Dimi obeyed Dad's instructions. In the early hours of the morning, before Mama had risen, he set out as the first light touched the rocky hillocks and barren stone plains beyond. Lucky darted ahead, tail wagging, while Dimi stepped cautiously around open shafts to reach their claim and check that everything seemed the same. The shaft beckoned temptingly. He was itching to get back down into the tunnel and find more of the colour.

A week after Dad had left, Dimi noticed that the knot on the windlass seemed slightly higher than usual. He carefully checked the mullock heaps, but it was impossible to tell if any of the pyramids of sandstone and loose rocks had shrunk or grown.

The next day, the winch knot seemed slightly lower than before. Dimi couldn't tell if it was his eyes playing tricks on him. What if a ratter was going down into their mine at night and stealing their precious opal?

The following morning, he left the dugout even earlier, while it was still dark. Dimi carried a lantern, a pick, candles, matches and the rope ladder. There were no sounds of pickaxes ringing or the creaking of buckets being cranked up to the surface. If he was quick, he could get down the shaft and take a swift look to check that no ratter had tried to raid it. As for bringing along the pick, he imagined how quickly Dad would forgive him if he were to return and discover that Dimi had found more colour ...

At the top of the shaft, Dimi told Lucky to stay and wait for him up on the surface. It was probably pointless; he doubted the pup would actually stay.

Despite Dimi's best efforts at training him, Lucky wasn't exactly obedient. The dog's attention was just as likely to be caught by a skittering lizard or someone opening a can of corned beef in a dugout on the other side of town.

Dimi hooked the rope ladder to the windlass

and proceeded to climb down to the tunnel where they had made their lucky strike. The candle burned brightly – the air was still good. He held the flame up close to the rock to see if he could determine if anyone else had been mining. It was difficult to tell.

And then he saw it up in the rocky ceiling: something gleaming. Colour!

Dimi lit two more candles and secured them on craggy ledges with melted wax. Just a few strikes, he promised himself. That was all. But as the rocks tumbled, there were more glimmerings of colour and Dimi lost himself in the thrill of discovery. There looked to be even more opal here than in the parcel of opal Dad had taken with him to the city. He struck again and again, dodging showers of scattering shale.

Just. One. More. Strike ...

There was no warning, only a sudden deafening rumble as the rock ceiling above collapsed. A shard struck Dimi on the temple, knocking him flat, at the same time a jumble of sand and stones buried his legs up to his thighs.

Dimi groaned. It was pitch black. He tried to shift his legs to pull them free, but the stabbing pains were unendurable. The rocks piled on top of them, like a dead weight.

The close darkness was terrifying. Dimi frantically felt the ground within his reach, patting rocks and dust in the darkness until finally his fingers scrabbled against the smooth, cold cylinder of an extinguished candle. He reached deep into his pocket, agonising pains running up his legs, and finally pulled the matches free.

When he lit the candle, any momentary relief of being able to see was destroyed by what was in front of him. There had been a cave-in.

The tunnel roof had collapsed, burying thc entrance under a mound of rocks and dirt that choked the entire passageway. The pick was nowhere to be seen. Even if it had been, Dimi was pinned to the ground, unable to sit up and start tugging away at the shale with his bare hands.

He wanted to scream and shout for help but he knew from living in the dugout how much the ground swallowed sound. No one would hear if he tried to cry out. And worse, because the tunnel was blocked, there was only a limited amount of air to breathe.

A cold creep of terror washed over him. Dad had ordered him not to go down into the mine. Lucky might be wandering about town and not return to the dugout until he was hungry. By the time Mama realised where Dimi was, it might be too late. There would be no air left to breathe.

He had to make a choice. Having light meant having less air. It was important to put out the candle to save what oxygen was left.

Casting another forlorn look at the wall of dirt and rocks blocking the tunnel and crushing his legs, Dimi blew out the candle and lay in the darkness.

In the myths Mama told him, only very few people got to return from the world beneath the ground – Hades.

Panicking would cause him to breathe faster and use more air. Dimi felt through the darkness to the smooth charm against his neck. The evil eye. For as long as Dimi could remember, it had nestled against Dad's chest. Now it lay cool against his own chest, deep beneath the earth. For all the shooting pain in his legs, Dimi was starting to feel sleepy. Was this how it felt to die?

Chapter 10

Enemy Rescue

Dimi awoke in darkness. Where was he? His head hurt and he couldn't feel his legs. What had woken him?

And then he heard it: a faint scratching. Had he dreamt it?

But no, there it was again. He listened, feeling dizzy and faint, as the scrabbling turned to scraping.

A faint beam of light lit the ceiling of the passage. Someone shouted through the thin gap between the dirt and tunnel roof. "Dimi? Dimi!"

"Here," he called weakly. "I'm here."

It seemed to take an eternity, but Dimi fixated on the faint beam of light as it grew wider and stronger.

He was unwilling to blink and miss a moment

as the top of the wall of earth was gradually shovelled and scraped away.

Finally, enough of the rockfall had been cleared for a figure to squeeze over the top and crawl across to Dimi. "I have you now," the man crooned in a musical voice, gently stroking Dimi's forehead. "You are safe." It was Frank. "But I must go to get help."

Dimi groaned. "Don't leave me, please!"

Frank shook his head, readying himself to clamber back out through the narrow hole he had dug between the rockfall and the tunnel's ceiling. "We will need more men to help get you free. I won't be long."

Dimi lay waiting. What if more rocks fell while Frank was gone? What if Frank had been lying and it suited him to let Dimi die in the hole, knowing that Dad would then probably abandon the claim?

Dimi would not have been able to say if it was hours or days before Frank returned. He brought with him a water bottle from which Dimi, parched, gratefully sipped.

Behind the rockfall came the sounds of shovelling and the creak of the windlass as buckets of debris were hauled away. When there was enough room to get into the passageway, several more men carefully shovelled away the rock litter crushing Dimi's legs. They had brought a stretcher and tenderly lifted Dimi onto it, before binding him to it tightly.

"Watch how you move him," one of them said. "Don't want the boy to end up paralysed. We're going to have to winch him up vertically. Otherwise, the stretcher won't fit through the shaft."

Outside, it was almost dark. Dimi blinked. Had he been trapped under the ground for the entire day?

"*Kardia mou*! My heart!" Mama rushed to the stretcher even as the men carried him to the wooden tray of a flatbed truck. Her large eyes were filled with tears. Beside her, Lucky turned circles, whining pitifully.

Frank helped Mama up onto the tray while Lucky leapt up. They sat on either side, keeping Dimi's stretcher steady as the truck slowly rumbled away. It rattled down to a large, flat area outside of the town where no shafts had been dug, and a motley assortment of cars and trucks were lined up in opposite rows with their headlights on.

"Everyone's lighting the runway for the flying doctor's plane," Frank explained. "Mrs Stein got on the radio as soon as we raised the alarm. She's been on it all day trying to get the plane to come sooner." He gestured to the surrounding cars and trucks. "The medical service said it was too dangerous for the plane to try to land in the dark, so Mrs Stein called in a few favours ..."

Sure enough, from above came the drone of a small plane.

It landed neatly between the twin rows of headlights before coming to a halt. Seemingly from nowhere, people materialised around the flatbed truck to race the stretcher across to the plane.

"What about Lucky?" Dimi murmured, still dazed and in increasing pain.

"I'll look after him for you," Frank reassured him. "He was the reason I came down to look for you. He was scratching at the top of your mine shaft and wouldn't stop barking. I'll keep an eye on the claim until you're back."

With that, Dimi closed his eyes and felt Mama squeeze his hand tenderly as the plane lifted into the air and the darkness.

Chapter 11

Belonging

Four months later, they finally arrived home in their own brand-new, shiny-blue truck that they'd bought in the city. It was a relief to not have to take a train and then camels! When they pulled up outside the dugout, Dad helped lift Dimi to the ground while Mama held out his crutches.

Dimi tentatively took a few steps across the stony ground with its litter of pebbles.

A truck rumbled through the dust behind them. Out climbed Frank. Close on his heels was Lucky – no longer a puppy but a young dog. Lucky leapt to greet Dimi with a flurry of licks, planting his outsized paws on Dimi's belly and causing him to stumble.

Dimi smiled shyly at Frank. "Thank you."

Frank winked and gave Lucky an affectionate pat. "Any time. He nearly ate me out of house and home."

Dad cleared his throat. "Er … I believe I owe you my thanks, too."

"It's nothing," Frank said. "You would have done the same for me. It can be lonely out here, and dangerous, like your boy discovered. We have to look out for each other."

Dad nodded. Then, taking a deep breath, he firmly shook Frank's hand before turning to Mama. He looked sheepish. "I thought maybe I could unload when it's a bit cooler and, er …"

Mama and Dimi exchanged a look. Opal fever. Dad's impatience with having to remain in the city over the past few months for Dimi's leg operations had become increasingly obvious.

He had sold their opal discovery for a good price. Now they had enough money for Mama to wear an exquisite, opal evil-eye necklace that Dad had paid a jeweller to fashion for her. It wasn't even totally necessary for them to return to the town, but Dad told them he felt as if he belonged out there, down in the ground, away from the crowd. And that there was still more opal to discover!

Stacked on the truck's flatbed tray was furniture, cooking pots and pans, and mattresses. If they were going to be in this strange underground desert town for some time, then Mama said they should be comfortable. There was even a small lemon tree in a pot that Mama was determined to keep alive.

She had also bought practical, hard-wearing cloth to sew clothes for the miners as a side business. But in amongst it was one bolt was one bolt of beautiful, silky blue fabric to make something nice for Mrs Stein at the post office. It was going to be a surprise. Mama had wept when she heard how the German woman had spent the better part of the day on the radio, chasing help for Dimi.

The things they had bought in the city were waiting to be unloaded, but they all knew that it was hardly going to rain.

Dimi rested while Mama started dusting and settling back in. The doctors had said that there was still a while to go before Dimi made a full recovery, but before long he'd be out there kicking a ball again like the best of them. Only, Dimi didn't care about kicking balls. Like Dad, he dreamt about one thing.

By the time he was able to walk without crutches and deemed ready to go back to the mine, Dimi was filled with nervous anticipation. Dad had since found some more colour in amongst the potch, but not as much as the first windfall.

It turned out that the cave-in had been caused when Dimi was mining in a tunnel directly beneath another abandoned shaft. There was only a thin layer of rock there and, under the force of Dimi's pick blows, it had inevitably collapsed. Frank had helped Dad to shore up the tunnel. In fact, the two men sometimes now worked together, with Frank coming around on Sundays to enjoy Mama's moussaka improvised from tin cans and whatever could be bought from the general store.

Dimi stood above the shaft, peering down into the dark depths of the single round hole, like the black pupil of his evil-eye charm. As he climbed down the rope ladder, he was surprised to feel no terror, only the cool and quiet. It was almost welcoming. Down below, when Dad lit the candles and they held them up to seams in the stone, Dimi's heart started to pound. But it wasn't from fear. There, gleaming out from the sandstone, was the faintest hint of colour.